MW00953248

Little Green Elephant Books
978-0-5788727-8-0

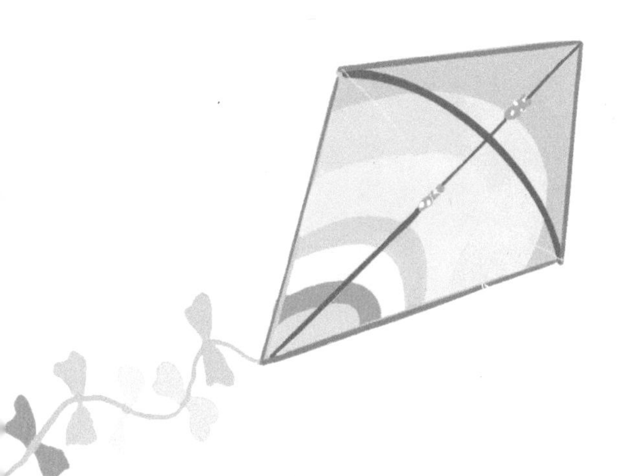

Flying High

BY DEBBIE MCLACHLAN

Illustrated by Christy Plummer

Dedicated to...

For my children, you are the reason
I believe in magic. - DM

For my grandchildren. - CP

You wake up one morning
ready to fly,
gaze out of your window
to the cloudy blue sky.

DREAM
big
LITTLE
one

A hummingbird flaps by
beating its wings,
you listen more closely
as your heart starts to sing.

Seizing your supplies you dash for the stairs,
chasing your dreams with no worries or cares.

Out towards the fields
where the wildflowers sow,
searching for the perfect
spot to let your heart grow.

It will take all you've got
to set this kite free,
you leap and you bounce
but it crashes by a tree!

You pick the kite up and spring to your feet,
you will *not* let this moment be one of defeat.

Suddenly a gust of wind whirls
through the cool crisp air.

The kite starts to tangle,
you fall deep into despair.

“I **will** fly this kite,”
you announce to the sun,
reaching for the string
to get the job done.

Running faster and faster you never give up.

“Perseverance,” you whisper,
“this will take more than good luck.”

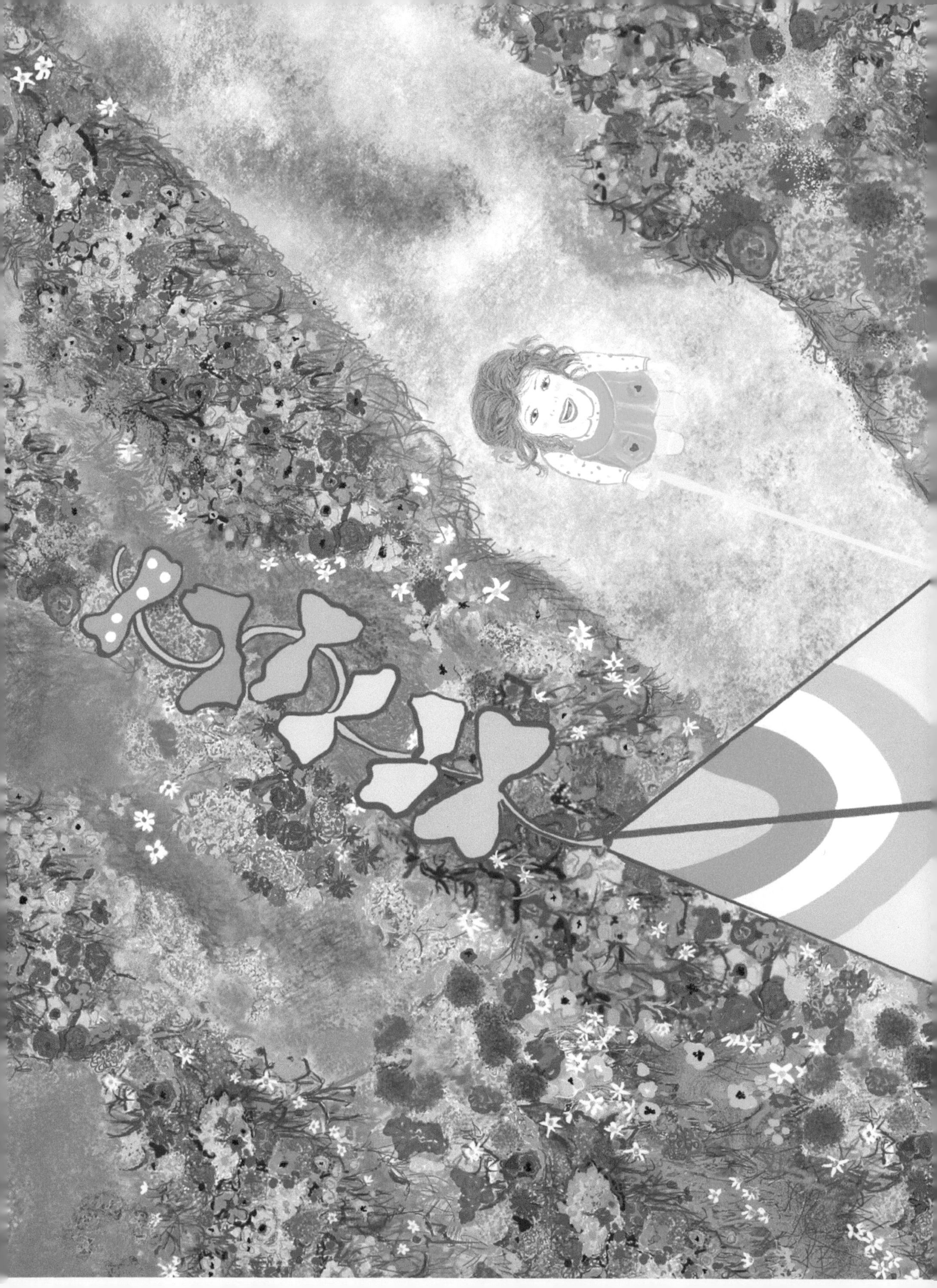

Higher and higher
the kite soars to the sky,
swooping and swirling
a skein of geese fly by.

You dance and you twirl
in great jubilation.
A rainbow appears
to join in celebration!

"I did it!" you exclaim
as you jump up with glee.
The kite is flying
and it's finally free.

With a spring in your step
you say farewell to the sun,
returning home peacefully
as you realize you have won.

Deep in slumber
you know you
tried your best,

and never
gave up
when put to
the test.

Always believe in chasing the sun.

Your dreams can come true...
just have faith little one.

CPSIA information can be obtained
at www.ICGtesting.com
Printed in the USA
LVHW071931230421
685408LV00009B/215

* 9 7 8 0 5 7 8 8 7 2 7 8 0 *